MEET THE CHARACTERS

SPIDEY

A SPECIAL SPIDER GAVE PETER PARKER SUPER POWERS. NOW HE FIGHTS VILLAINS AS SPIDEY!

MILES MORALES

MILES MORALES IS ALWAYS READY TO LEAP INTO ACTION. HE CAN TURN INVISIBLE!

GHOST-SPIDER

GWEN STACY IS SUPER SMART. AS GHOST-SPIDER, SHE CAN GLIDE ON HER WEB-WINGS.

MS. MARVEL

MS. MARVEL IS A YOUNG SUPER HERO. WHEN SHE SAYS "EMBIGGEN," SHE CAN STRETCH HER ARMS AND LEGS!

GREEN GOBLIN

GREEN GOBLIN PLAYS TRICKS! HE FLIES ON A GOBLIN GLIDER AND THROWS PUMPKIN PRANKS.

DOC OCK

DOC OCK IS VERY SMART. SHE WANTS TO TAKE OVER THE CITY WITH HER METAL TENTACLES.

RHINO

RHINO IS BIG AND STRONG. HE LIKES TO RUN AND BREAK THINGS.

HOW TO READ A COMIC

Follow our easy guide, and you will be reading comics in no time!

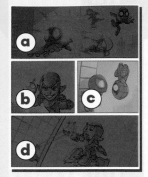

1 EACH PAGE OF A COMIC IS MADE UP OF PICTURES, OR PANELS. EACH PANEL TELLS ONE PART OF THE STORY.

2 THE CHARACTERS SPEAK IN WORD BALLOONS. THE POINTER OR TAIL AT THE END OF THE BALLOON SHOWS WHO IS SPEAKING.

3 SOMETIMES YOU WILL SEE WORDS IN A BOX. THAT IS CALLED A CAPTION. CAPTIONS HELP TELL THE STORY AND TELL YOU THINGS YOU NEED TO KNOW, LIKE TIME OR LOCATION.

4 READ THE PANELS FROM LEFT TO RIGHT AND TOP TO BOTTOM. FOLLOW THE ARROWS ABOVE, AND YOU WILL SEE WHAT WE MEAN.

5 NOW SWING ON AND READ!

TIC-TAC-TRACE-E!

SOON...

YOU **WON, TRACE-E!**

SEE? *ANYONE* CAN PLAY THE GAME!

BEEP!

WHERE IS SHE GOING?

BEEP! BEEP!

LATER, IN PETER'S ROOM...

ANYONE CAN PLAY!

WELL, MAYBE NOT ANYONE...

BEEP?

THE END!

8

GOO TIMES!

TEAM SPIDEY IS ON WATCH.

HELP!

WHAT IS THE PROBLEM?

WE ARE HAVING A **CUPCAKE** PARTY.

WHERE ARE THE CUPCAKES?

THAT IS THE PROBLEM!

THE CUPCAKES NEVER ARRIVED...

BECAUSE OF **HIM**!

IT IS **GREEN GOBLIN**!

WHERE DID YOU GET THAT CUPCAKE, **GOBBY**?

FROM MY NEW FRIEND...

...THE DELIVERY PERSON!

HE TRAPPED ME IN **GOBLIN GOO**!

11

LOST AND FOUND!

WOW!

I WILL USE MY SPIDER-STRENGTH!

THANKS, GHOST-SPIDER!

WHERE ARE YOU GOING NOW?

I LOST MY HEADPHONES.

SO I AM TRYING TO **FIND** THEM.

LOOK NO FURTHER!

ELECTRONIC

YOU CAN HAVE **THESE** HEADPHONES!

THANK YOU!

THIS IS THE **ONLY** WAY TO WEB-SWING!

THE END!

ART CLUB!

TODAY, AT THE **WEB-QUARTERS**＊.

WELCOME TO **ART CLUB!**

THIS IS FUN, MILES!

BEEP!

I'M PAINTING A PICTURE OF MYSELF!

I'M PAINTING MY DRUM KIT!

BEEP!

I'M PAINTING **AUNT MAY.**

THE END!

PLAY BALL!

SPIDEY GETS AN **ALERT***!

NEWS FLASH!

BASEBALLS ARE FLYING EVERYWHERE...

...AND BREAKING THINGS!

BEEP!

I AM ON THE CASE!

SOON...

WHERE ARE THOSE BASEBALLS COMING FROM?

WHOOSH!

THERE GOES ONE NOW!

SPIDEY CHECKS THE PARK.

NO ONE IS PLAYING BASEBALL HERE.

SUDDENLY...

CLUNK!

OH, NO! I'VE BEEN STACKING CANS ALL MORNING!

I WILL BE BACK TO HELP YOU.

ANYONE WHO HITS BASEBALLS THAT FAR...

MUST BE **VERY** STRONG!

AHA!

WHACK!

THE END!

WHERE'S HULK?

THE SPIDEY TEAM IS HAVING A PARTY FOR HULK!

THE PLACE LOOKS GREAT!

IT SURE DOES!

BEEP!

LOOK AT THIS PICTURE I MADE FOR HULK!

HE WILL LOVE IT, MILES!

surprise, **HULK!**

HULK HAS BEEN **SAD** LATELY.

NO ONE EVER THREW HIM A **SURPRISE PARTY** BEFORE.

THIS WILL CHEER HIM UP!

OUR OTHER GUESTS WILL BRING HULK HERE.

BEEP!

GREETINGS!

HI, SPIDEY!

BLACK PANTHER! MS. MARVEL! IT IS GOOD TO SEE YOU!

LOOK AT THAT TALL GARBAGE TRUCK!

MAYBE **HULK** IS LIFTING IT.

THAT IS NOT HULK. IT IS **RHINO**!

WHY ARE YOU STEALING A GARBAGE TRUCK?

PLAYING WITH TRUCKS IS FUN!

SILLY RHINO!

LET'S PUT THE GARBAGE TRUCK BACK!

DO YOU SEE HULK?

NO, BUT I SEE A BIG BALL! MAYBE HULK IS THROWING IT?

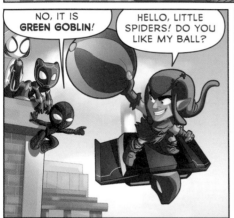

NO, IT IS **GREEN GOBLIN!**

HELLO, LITTLE SPIDERS! DO YOU LIKE MY BALL?

IT IS FILLED WITH **GOBLIN GOO.**

HAVE A CLOSER LOOK!

I DO NOT THINK SO.

POP!

MY BALL!

I WAS GOING TO USE THAT ROBOT TO COMMIT CRIMES!

NOT THIS TIME!

BUT WHERE IS **HULK**?

BACK AT WEB-QUARTERS...

HULK!

WHERE WERE YOU?

I **OVERHEARD** YOU TALKING ABOUT MY PARTY. I WAS SO EXCITED, I GOT **YOU** A SURPRISE!

GREEN PICKLES! **NOW** IT IS A PARTY!

THE END!

32

MUSIC TIME!

GWEN PLAYS THE DRUMS AT THE WEB-QUARTERS!

CRASH!

THUMP!

BOOM!

THAT WAS GREAT, GWEN!

WAS THAT A NEW SONG?

IT SURE WAS!

WOULD YOU LIKE TO PLAY IT, TOO?

YES! BUT WE DO NOT HAVE DRUMS.

HMMM...

I HAVE AN IDEA!

WE JUST NEED THESE WASTE BASKETS!

I GET IT! WE CAN TURN THEM...

INTO DRUMS!

SOON...

YOU GUYS MAKE THE SONG SOUND EVEN BETTER!

BOOM!

THUMP!

THE END!

LOOKING FOR CLUES!

"YOU FOUND A NEW CLUE! AND YOU MET A PUPPY."

"GO GET SOME ICE CREAM NEXT TO THE GUPPY."

GUPPIES ARE FISH!

SOON...

THIS MUST BE THE PLACE!

PETS & FISH

ICE CREAM

THERE'S **ICE CREAM**, AND A **GUPPY**!

INSIDE...

GHOST-SPIDER LEFT THIS FOR YOU.

THANK YOU!

IT IS OUR NEXT **CLUE**!

"GO AND FIND A HELPING HAND."

"THEN TAKE A SEAT AND SIT IN THE SAND!"

I THINK I HAVE IT!

A LITTLE LATER, AT THE BEACH...

WELCOME TO YOUR SURPRISE!

WOW-- LOOK AT **THAT**!

TA-DA! THANKS FOR YOUR HELP, MS. MARVEL.

A DAY AT THE BEACH WITH FRIENDS IS THE **BEST** SURPRISE!

I AM ALWAYS GLAD TO LEND A **HAND**!

THE END!

38

WHERE'S RHINO?

MILES SWINGS ABOVE THE CITY.

IT IS A NICE DAY!

SUDDENLY...

MY SPIDEY-SENSE* IS TINGLING!

HELP!

WHOA!

IT LOOKS LIKE **RHINO** WAS HERE.

HE SURE WAS!

OR CHEESE!

HE WENT THROUGH THE TOY STORE!

I WILL FIND YOU SOON, RHINO!

THERE IS RHINO!

AND HE IS...GETTING ICE CREAM?

WHY DID YOU RUN THROUGH ALL THOSE STORES, RHINO?

I **LOVE** ICE CREAM!

WHEN I HEARD THE SOUND OF THE ICE CREAM TRUCK...

I CAME **RUNNING**!

NEXT TIME, YOU SHOULD GO **AROUND** THE BUILDINGS...

NOT **THROUGH** THEM!

OOPS. SORRY! I WILL CLEAN UP MY MESS!

THE END!

THE MISSING BOOK MYSTERY!

RAINY-DAY HEROES!

GHOST-SPIDER AND MILES PLAY GAMES WITH MS. MARVEL IN THE PARK!

GET READY, MS. MARVEL.

HERE IT COMES!

OOPS! I THREW IT TOO HIGH.

DO NOT WORRY!

I CAN STRETCH...

AND CATCH IT!

YOUR STRETCHING POWER SURE IS GREAT!

YOU MIGHT EVEN SAY...

IT COMES IN **HANDY**!

CATCH, GHOST-SPIDER!

WAY TO USE YOUR WEBS, MILES!

thwip!

UH-OH. IT IS STARTING TO **RAIN**!

46

WE SHOULD GET OUT OF THE RAIN!

I THINK I CAN HELP!

IF I MAKE MY HANDS BIG ENOUGH...

I CAN COVER YOU BOTH!

BUT **YOU** ARE STILL GETTING WET!

THE END!

AN ALARMING* SITUATION!

PETER'S ALARM WAKES HIM UP!

YAWN!

RING! RING!

CAN YOU TURN OFF THE ALARM, TRACE-E?

BEEP!

RING! RING!

THAT IS STRANGE.

IT WILL NOT TURN OFF.

MEOW!

RING! RING!

TRACE-E COVERS THE ALARM WITH A PILLOW.

RING! RING!

I UNPLUGGED THE CLOCK. BUT IT IS **STILL** RINGING.

RING!

RING!

PETER HAS AN IDEA. HE LOOKS FOR SOMETHING...

RING! RING!

AHA! THERE IT IS.

I USED THIS GADGET ONCE...

...TO STOP DOC OCK'S OCTOBOTS!

IT CAN TURN OFF THE ALARM!

NOW IT IS **QUIET!**

THE END!

HELPFUL HULK!

HULK WANTS TO HELP THE SPIDEY TEAM!

HELLO, FRIENDS!

HEY, HULK!

CAN I HELP YOU?

WE ARE TRYING TO FIGURE OUT WHERE TO PUT SOMETHING.

BUT WE CANNOT DECIDE WHERE IT SHOULD GO!

I CAN DO THAT!

I WILL PUT **THIS** OVER HERE!

WAIT, HULK!

AND I WILL PUT **THIS** OVER HERE!

YOU DO NOT UNDERSTAND!

NOW YOU SHOULD HAVE **ROOM!**

BUT, HULK...

...WE WERE ONLY TRYING TO DECIDE WHERE TO PUT THIS **FAN!**

OOPS! NEXT TIME, I WILL **LISTEN** BEFORE I HELP!

THE END!

54

SEND IN THE CLONES*!

THERE IS TROUBLE AT THE ZOO!

OH, NO--IT IS **DOC OCK**!

NOW WHY DON'T YOU BE A GOOD GUARD...

...AND STAY OUT OF MY WAY?

HELP!

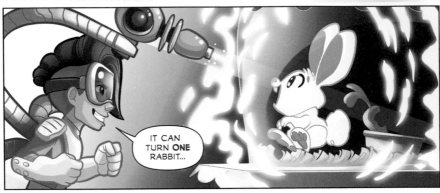

MEANWHILE...

OKAY, LITTLE ONES!

OH, NO! MY CARROT!

WHO WANTS TO GO...

...FOR A **RIDE**?

LET'S GET YOU BACK TO THE RABBIT EXHIBIT!

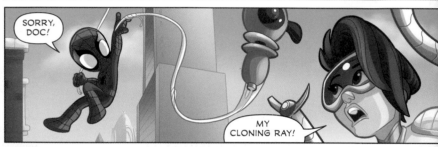

THE END!

VOCABULARY WORDS

Some words in the *Spidey and His Amazing Friends* stories are marked with a ∗. Here is a list of those words and their meanings:

Gliding – Moving in an easy way

WEB-Quarters – Team Spidey's secret base

Alert – A warning

Clue – Something that helps lead to solving a mystery

Spidey-sense – A feeling that warns Spidey, Ghost-Spider, and Miles of danger

Exits – When someone leaves a place

Thwip – The action of shooting a web

Alarming – Worrying

Clones – Copies of something

Ray – A wave of energy

Capture – To catch something or someone

Script by **Steve Behling**
Layouts and cleans by **Giovanni Rigano, Antonello Dalena**
Inks by **Cristina Giorgilli, Cristina Stella**
Color by **Dario Calabria, Lucio De Giuseppe**
Cover and design by **David Roe**